ISBN: 9781838147419

Maybe the Moon
London, UK

Corona

(the germ)

by Sophie Morris
Illustrated by Taryn Kosviner

Once upon a time there was a little germ
called Corona who lived in the mouth of a bat.

All day long, Corona
slept on bat's...

hairy
tongue

But once the sun set,
Corona soared through the night.

One evening, bat swooped down
to the river to quench her thirst.

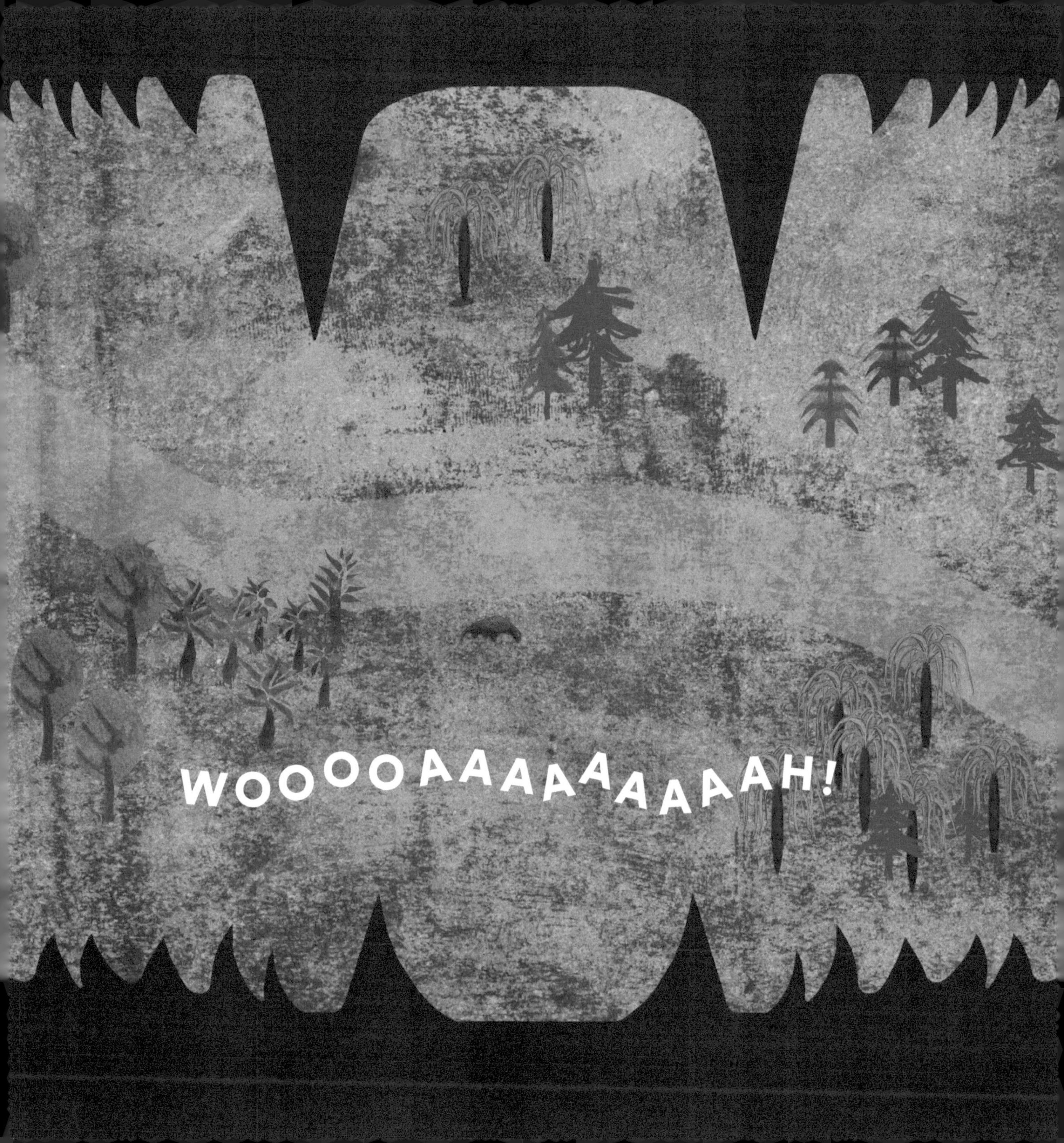
WOOOOOAAAAAAAAAAAH!

Cough
Splutter

Splat!

What happened? Where was he?
All Corona could see was
a mountain of spikes.

It felt hard and cold.
His heart sank.

He had landed on Pangolin,
the shy creature he had spotted
during his night time adventures.

Corona wanted to curl up into a tight ball, just like Pangolin did when he was frightened. He missed bat terribly.

Would he ever fly again?

But soon enough, something
extraordinary happened.

The sun rose

Corona had never
seen the day before.

**LOOK HOW BRIGHT
EVERYTHING IS!**

He was spellbound.
Maybe it wouldn't be
too bad after all.

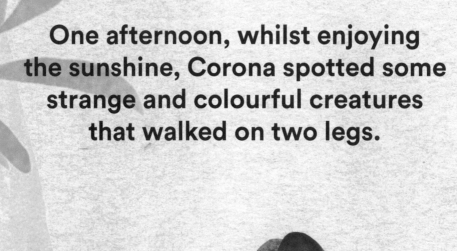

One afternoon, whilst enjoying
the sunshine, Corona spotted some
strange and colourful creatures
that walked on two legs.

'Hey guys. Look at this big
round pinecone.'

Ouch!

Suddenly everything felt strange again.
What happened? Where was he?

And then Corona realised.
He was on the skin of one
of the humans.

Before he knew it, the world was
racing past him. Corona felt dizzy
with excitement!

Squelch

Oh no! What's happened now?

HEY!
WAIT FOR ME!

...he yelled. But of course humans
cannot hear tiny germ voices.

Just when he thought that his
adventure was over...

Y_IK_ES !

...another hand swept him
up and off he went.

WOW!

WHAT A VIEW!

And just like that Corona
travelled from person to person
and place to place.

He couldn't believe how lucky
these humans were.

They could do the most
marvelous things.

And now...

WOOOHOOO!

...so could he.

He felt on top of the world!

Then, almost overnight, everything changed.
The world looked very different.
Corona was confused.

Where did all the people go?
Why did they look so worried?
Everything felt strange and scary.

He felt all wobbly inside and even
tinier than usual.

Corona screamed
and burst into tears.

ARE THE PEOPLE
CROSS WITH ME?

IS THIS MY FAULT?

Corona missed his fun adventures.
In this slow and quiet world,
his worries were too loud.

But then, just when
everything felt too much,
Corona noticed something
else had begun to change.

Somehow, his rapid travels
across the world had
magically connected
everybody's hearts.

Far and wide, *wonderful things* were happening.

Kind-hearted helpers
emerged, big and small.

Even the penguins did their part, keeping the other sea creatures company.

With their hearts connected, the people
felt more for each other than ever before.

OHHHHHH!

Corona finally understood.

The best thing about humans isn't
all the fun things they can DO,
it's the way they can BE there
for each other.

Just with a look, or a smile or a nod.

Corona had so many stories but no one to share them with. Perhaps he didn't belong with humans after all?

Splash!

WOOOOOAAAAH!

Was he back on the water slide?!

WOOOOAAH!

'Welcome' said
a calm, kind voice.

For the first time in his life,
Corona was seen and heard.

AAAAAAAHHHHHHHH!

Corona breathed a long sigh of relief.
His whole body softened.

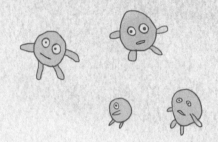

Corona spent the rest of his days
floating about, surrounded
by his new germ friends.

**And to his surprise,
he had never felt happier.**

CPSIA information can be obtained
at www.ICGtesting.com
Printed in the USA
LVHW070957100920
665516LV00016B/320